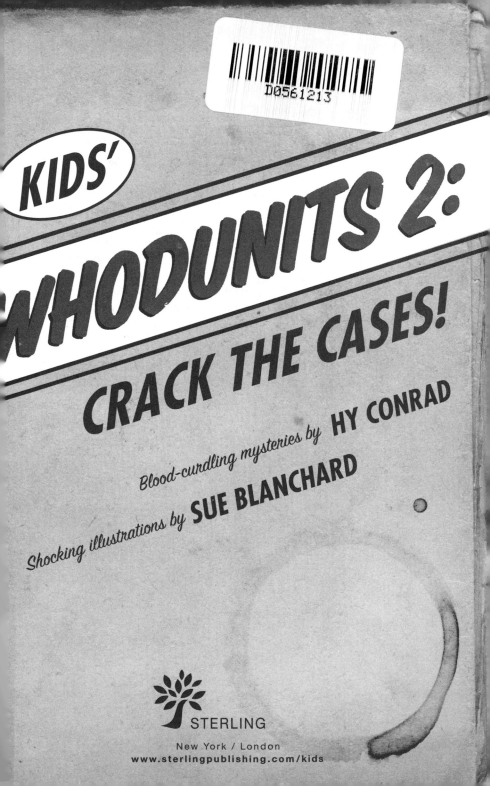

KIDS'

WHODUNITS 2:

CRACK THE CASES!

Blood-curdling mysteries by **HY CONRAD**

Shocking illustrations by **SUE BLANCHARD**

STERLING

New York / London

www.sterlingpublishing.com/kids

Dedicated to:

JEFF JOHNSON,
FOR THINGS TOO NUMEROUS TO MENTION

STERLING and the distinctive Sterling logo are registered trademarks of
Sterling Publishing Co., Inc.

Library of Congress Cataloging-in-Publication Data

Conrad, Hy.
  Kids' whodunits 2 : crack the cases! / by Hy Conrad ; illustrations by Sue Blanchard.
      p. cm. — (Jonah Bixby mysteries)
  ISBN 978-1-4027-5398-5
  1. Puzzles—Juvenile literature. 2. Detective and mystery stories--Juvenile literature. I. Blanchard,
Susan, ill. II. Title.

GV1507.D4C66725 2009
793.73--dc22

2008022433

2 4 6 8 10 9 7 5 3 1

Published by Sterling Publishing Co., Inc.
387 Park Avenue South, New York, NY 10016
Text © 2009 by Hy Conrad
Illustrations © 2009 by Sue Blanchard
Distributed in Canada by Sterling Publishing
c/o Canadian Manda Group, 165 Dufferin Street
Toronto, Ontario, Canada M6K 3H6
Distributed in the United Kingdom by GMC Distribution Services
Castle Place, 166 High Street, Lewes, East Sussex, England BN7 1XU
Distributed in Australia by Capricorn Link (Australia) Pty. Ltd.
P.O. Box 704, Windsor, NSW 2756, Australia

Manufactured in the United States of America

Sterling ISBN 978-1-4027-5398-5

Designed by Lauren Rille

For information about custom editions, special sales, premium and corporate purchases,
please contact Sterling Special Sales Department at 800-805-5489
or specialsales@sterlingpublishing.com.

CONTENTS

HOW DOES A TWELVE-YEAR-OLD become a detective, solving real cases for a real police department? For Jonah Bixby, it began with family. Both his mother and his father had been detectives in the Major Crimes division, so he probably got a lot of his skill from them. But then when Jonah was five, his father was killed in the line of duty.

After her husband's death, Carol Bixby thought about leaving the force in order to focus on raising her son. But Jonah knew his mother loved her work, and he was already the unofficial mascot of the Fifth Precinct. So, before anyone realized what was happening, Jonah eased into a unique type of childcare and his mother decided to keep her job.

From the first grade on, Jonah received a second, more informal education after school. Some of the best detectives in the state acted as his babysitters. Jonah practiced his reading on the police department's wanted posters. He sharpened his pattern-recognition skills by flipping through books full of mug shots. And at naptime, Jonah was probably the only kid in Indiana who nodded off to true crime stories, thinly disguised as fairy tales.

The result was that Jonah was already breaking cases by the time he was halfway through elementary school. Not officially, of course. But he had a certain way of looking at things, of finding the one simple clue that could unravel a complicated crime. His mother tried to keep it all low-key, since the city authorities would frown on this type of civilian help. But half the department knew that if you were stuck on a tricky case, you might want to talk to the twelve-year-old doing his homework in the interrogation room.

v

JONAH AND THE SICK SWAN

"I'M NOT A BABYSITTER," Officer Oliphant grumbled as he led Jonah out of the precinct house and toward his patrol cruiser.

"Hey, I'm twelve," Jonah said. But he knew what the officer meant. For two Saturdays in a row, while his mother was busy working a case, Jonah had been handed off to the young patrolman. Officer Tom Oliphant, straight out of the academy, was sensitive about getting assigned the most menial jobs, including looking after a senior detective's son. "I don't like this either, sir."

But he actually did like it. In the morning, they patrolled the streets and wrote up tickets. Jonah was pretty good at spotting illegally parked cars. And the afternoon would prove to be even better. Jonah would get a cool puzzle to solve, and Oliphant would wind up with a commendation. The officer would never again complain about babysitting Jonah.

It all began after a lunch of drive-thru burgers. "I have to pick up the mail," Oliphant sighed, as he put the cruiser into drive and turned down Glendale Street. He explained as he drove. "You've heard of Jackson Pyle, right?"

"Sure," Jonah said, "the escaped killer. He dug a tunnel out of Indiana State Penitentiary and no one's seen him since."

"Yeah," Oliphant said. "Well, his mother lives here in Beaverton. We have a phone tap and a running warrant on her mail. So, every day, I get to drive up to her mailbox and check to see if Pyle sent her anything."

"Seems like a long shot." Jonah tried not to sound critical.

"Maybe. But Jackson and his mom used to be tight. We know he's been in touch with her. She accidentally let that slip out."

"Maybe he's e-mailing her."

Oliphant shook his head. "She doesn't have access to a computer. But there are other ways. For instance, he could buy a disposable phone and she could call him from a pay phone somewhere. We couldn't tap a call like that."

They had just turned off onto a rural road. A minute later, the officer slowed down and pulled off to the shoulder. There was a lone mailbox, separated from the house by an overgrown hedge. "Pyle" was printed on the side in stick-on letters. Oliphant got out of the car, walked around, and opened the mailbox.

"This is so useless," he muttered, leafing through the small collection of bills and junk mail. But then he found a postcard and stopped.

From the passenger seat, Jonah could see it in the officer's hand. It was a picture postcard, the kind you could buy in a thousand tourist shops. On one side was the skyline of Manhattan and the printed words, "Wish You Were Here!" On the blank side was a simple handwritten message.

Oliphant read it aloud: "I'll be here for the next few days. I don't know if you want to talk, but I hope you can force heaven to hate one sick swan." That was all it said. No signature and no return address.

"It's from him," Jonah said in a breathy whisper.

Oliphant nodded. "Pyle obviously knows we're checking her mail. But what does it mean? 'Force heaven to hate one sick swan.'"

"Why does he want heaven to hate a swan?" Jonah asked.

"It must be some kind of prearranged code," Oliphant said. "We'll send this to the FBI." He turned the card at an angle and looked along its surface. "Pyle never struck me as an intellectual. I just hope we decipher it before he moves on."

Jonah took one more look at the words. He mumbled them aloud several times and then smiled.

"I know what it means."

WHAT DOES THE POSTCARD MESSAGE MEAN?

TURN TO PAGE 80 FOR THE SOLUTION TO "JONAH AND THE SICK SWAN."

THROWING THE GAME

"ANGIE, HI. You going to Brad's party on Saturday?" Jonah had been practicing the line all morning, but it still sounded lame. He wasn't really asking a ninth-grader on a date, he told himself, just inquiring if she was going to a party.

"No, I scored something better," Angie said, oblivious to the whole date question. She reached into her bag and a second later pulled out a ticket. "The concert in Indianapolis. Can you believe it? I called Monday, right at six in the morning. I can't believe I got through. The radio says they were sold out in twenty minutes."

Jonah didn't know the band she mentioned, but he knew it was Angie's favorite. The ticket and her enthusiasm both seemed genuine, so he didn't feel too bad. It wasn't the same as a real rejection. Middle school, he was starting to learn, was hard.

"Jonah Bixby?" It was Principal Daly, coming up behind him and grabbing him by the shoulder. "Can we talk for a minute?"

All thoughts of Angie fled from his mind as Jonah followed the principal into his office and took a seat across from the big desk. "Am I in trouble?" he asked, his mouth as dry as sand.

"Not at all," said Principal Daly and closed the door behind him. "Jonah, I need you to do a little investigating."

Jonah didn't know how they'd found out, but the news of Jonah's special skill had reached the school administration. "You can say no, of course. But let me just tell you what our problem is."

The principal grabbed a remote, pressed a button, and the TV on top of his bookcase sprang to life. Jonah instantly recognized the jumpy image. It was yesterday's basketball game. The girls' senior team had played their last game of the season, losing a squeaker to St. Anthony's, a nearby Catholic school. Jonah had been there himself, partly out of school spirit and partly to watch Angie, the center, run up and down the court.

"We heard a rumor that one of the players was cheating. Throwing the game."

"You mean losing on purpose?" This was hard for Jonah to fathom. Basketball was almost an Indiana religion. True, the girls' team wasn't great this year. But if they'd won this one, they would have gone to the regionals in Evansville this weekend. And that was pretty big.

"I've been eye-balling this all morning," Principal Daly continued. "The two forwards are our most obvious suspects." He stopped the tape and pointed to a tall blonde who had just missed a shot. "That's Molly Wrangel. She played for St. Anthony's last year before her folks switched her over to public school."

Jonah knew Molly, vaguely. She was a bit of a loner and seemed pretty resentful of her parents' decision. They silently watched a minute more of the tape and saw Molly foul the opposing guard, sending her to the free-throw line for two points.

"That guard was Molly's best friend at St. Anthony's," the principal pointed out. "And Molly fouled her three times last night."

When he aimed the remote and froze the image again, they were staring at the other forward. "That's Georgia Baker. I'm not telling any secrets when I say she's a borderline student. Academically. Her father doesn't help. He's kind of a lowlife. Arrested last year for running a book. You know what that is?"

Of course, Jonah knew. "Being a bookie," he answered. "Taking illegal bets."

"Right. It's silly to think anyone would bet on middle school basketball games, much less fix them. But this is Indiana."

Jonah nodded. He remembered seeing Georgia out behind the school one day last fall, playing poker with some older boys, high school age probably, winning a hand and laughing and taking their money.

"I don't want to go to the police. But I just can't ignore it. If I knew who it was, I could talk to her." Principal Daly switched off the set and turned to face his twelve-year-old student. "You don't have to help, Jonah. It's a lot, asking you to skulk around and spy on people."

"I won't skulk and spy."

"I understand," the principal said. "Well, thanks anyway."

"No, I mean I won't have to spy. I know who it is."

WHO IS THE CHEATING PLAYER?
WHAT CLUE TIPPED OFF JONAH?

TURN TO PAGE 80 FOR THE SOLUTION TO "THROWING THE GAME."

THE KIDNAPPER'S MISTAKE

JONAH AND HIS MOTHER walked from their car up the dark path to the front door. There was no moon and the house was isolated, a block from the nearest streetlamp. But they were guided by the lights from inside. Through the picture window, they could see a woman pacing the living room. A few feet away, a man in a suit sat with a glass of red wine. When Detective Bixby pushed the doorbell, it took them by surprise.

"Thanks for coming," the woman said as she ushered them inside. Her brows furrowed when she saw the twelve-year-old boy.

"Your call came just as we were leaving the movies," Carol Bixby explained. "You can talk in front of Jonah. He's very mature."

"Not a problem," Mrs. Granger said, although she seemed a little reluctant to go on. "Um, I just wanted to tell you in person. We paid the ransom."

Jonah already knew the basics. Last night Maryanne Granger's husband had been kidnapped. Against the advice of the family lawyer, she notified the police. Carol and her colleagues had advised her not to pay the ransom, at least until they could set a trap. It was standard procedure.

"This is my fault," said the man with the wine. "I talked Maryanne into paying it." Jonah assumed that he was the family lawyer. "The voice on the phone said to leave the money bag taped to the underside of the Jasper Park Bridge. I made the delivery myself about two hours ago. I thought about hiding nearby to see who picked it up, but I didn't want to endanger Marvin's life."

"You did the right thing," Mrs. Granger assured him.

But it didn't look that way to Jonah. They'd just paid an unknown kidnapper half a million dollars and had nothing to show for it.

"Where did you get the money so quickly?" his mother asked them.

"Marvin's company," said the lawyer. "He's their chief bio-tech scientist and they couldn't afford to lose him. The board authorized the funds this morning. We told them we were working with the police, but now... half a million dollars and those crooks still have Marvin."

"We'll check out Jasper Park," Carol said, reaching for her cell phone. "We might be lucky and find a witness who saw the pickup—or maybe some fingerprints. There's still a chance . . ."

But before she could dial the call, the front door creaked open. "Marvin!" Mrs. Granger nearly screamed the name, then ran to the mud-covered man in the doorway and hugged him.

"They dropped me on the other side of the woods." He coughed out the words. "I've been stumbling around forever trying to get here."

Five minutes later, Marvin Granger was sipping a cup of hot tea and giving Detective Bixby his statement. "Last night, I was home alone."

"I do volunteer work at the library every Tuesday night," his wife added.

"That's right," Marvin continued. "I was here in the living room reading a book when I looked out and saw a man on the lawn, just standing there. Without thinking, I opened the front door. I was barely outside when someone came from the side and hit me. I was knocked unconscious."

"So, there were two of them," Carol suggested.

"I guess," Marvin answered. "I was blindfolded from the moment I woke up until they dropped me off. No one ever spoke."

"Do you have any idea where they kept you?"

"I think it was someplace nearby. Maybe on the north end."

"That's right by Jasper Park," said the lawyer, "where I dropped off the ransom."

"Mom?" Jonah pretended to yawn. "I'm bored. Can I go out to the car?"

Carol looked at her son and figured it out almost instantly. "Excuse us just a minute," she told the Grangers and their lawyer. "Sorry."

A few seconds later and they were outside on the dark porch. "All right, young man. What's up?"

"I didn't know how else to get you alone," Jonah said apologetically. "Mom, something's wrong with their story. One of them is lying."

WHO IS LYING?
HOW DID JONAH KNOW?
TURN TO PAGE 81 FOR THE SOLUTION TO "THE KIDNAPPER'S MISTAKE."

THE TRILBY GHOST

"ARE YOU KIDS GOING to be all right on your own?" Sally Smith's father was putting on his jacket and heading for the door. "I have to go show the Trilby mansion."

Jonah and Sally were on the Smiths' living room rug, absorbed in their third hour of Risk. Sally bolted to her feet. "Can we come along?"

Jonah was on his feet, too. "Please? We won't be a bother." Even though he had just pushed his army halfway across Europe, Jonah was willing to put the board game on hold in order to finally get inside that house.

The Trilby mansion was the closest thing around to a haunted house. It was a huge Victorian ruin situated on a hill above the old cemetery. When old Mr. Trilby died two years ago, the Smith Real Estate Company was chosen to sell the property. But the mansion was in such bad shape that Mr. Smith had never been able to find a buyer, not until now.

Five minutes later and all three were in the car, driving up Hillside Road. "Amanda Grant is very excited about buying it." Mr. Smith sounded pretty excited himself. "She wants to take one more look before making an offer."

"She doesn't mind about the ghost?" asked Sally.

"Nonsense," her father said as he turned off the road and started up the winding driveway. "Who told you there's a ghost?"

"Our friend, Evan," Jonah answered. "He lives there, so he ought to know. He says the mansion is haunted by some Trilby ancestor who won't let anybody buy it."

Mr. Smith frowned. "Of course he'd say it's haunted. Evan's parents came to us two years ago, when the house was first empty. They offered to be the caretakers. They don't do much caretaking, but they get to live there rent-free. The last thing they want is for someone to finally kick them out."

As they pulled up to the front, they could see Amanda Grant, a petite, nervous-looking woman, waiting for them in the driveway. "Don't say anything about Evan's ghost," Mr. Smith warned.

Ms. Grant seemed nice enough. She shook hands with Sally and Jonah, and had no problem with them joining her inside. They were just about to go in when a pickup truck roared up and came to a squealing halt, its front tires resting right on top of a garden hose that snaked around the side of the mansion.

Evan's father, Amos Delido, hopped out of the truck. "Well, I see you're back for another look," he said to Ms. Grant. "Hope you got lots of money to fix it up." And with a nasty laugh, he skipped up the front steps.

Mr. Smith led them on a quick tour of the downstairs rooms. Most of them were unused by the current residents, the furniture covered in dust and the corners seemingly held together with cobwebs. Jonah thought it was the coolest. Sally wasn't so sure.

They climbed to the top of the grand staircase and were just starting down a hallway when Ms. Grant let out a scream. There, at the far end of the shadowy hall, stood the ghost. It was a flowing white apparition, flickering in the glow of a candle in its hand. Seconds later, the candle blew out and the ghost vanished back into the shadows.

Amanda Grant was the first one down the stairs. "I'm sorry." Her voice was shaking. "I can't buy a haunted house. My heart won't take it."

"It isn't haunted," Mr. Smith insisted. "It was one of the people who live here. They're trying to scare you."

The commotion had drawn Amos Delido and his wife into the front hallway. "I see you met the ghost," Amos chortled. "And don't think it was me. I was downstairs with my train set." That seemed believable to Jonah. As they were touring the main floor, he'd heard the train whistle coming up from the basement.

"Hi," Evan said with a crooked smile. The teenager had just come in. Jonah told him about the ghost and asked him where he'd been for the past few minutes. "I was out back, watering the garden. I just stopped when I heard the scream."

Evan's mother, Fanny Delido, also had an alibi. "I was making dinner," she claimed. The smell of cooking from the kitchen seemed to verify her story. "I know you don't want to believe it, Ms. Grant, but this house is haunted. Personally, we don't mind the ghost..."

Sally pulled Jonah aside and whispered in his ear. "One of them put on a sheet and played the ghost. I know it."

"So do I," Jonah whispered back.

WHICH DELIDO WAS MASQUERADING AS THE GHOST? HOW DID JONAH SEE THROUGH THE CULPRIT'S ALIBI?

TURN TO PAGE 81 FOR THE SOLUTION TO "THE TRILBY GHOST."

A BIXBY THANKSGIVING

"IT'S SO BITTERLY cold," Aunt Delia complained as she took off her fur coat and handed it to Jonah. "Am I the first one? Hmmph, the invitation said two P.M. But the Bixby relatives are always late, aren't they? Be a good boy and put this somewhere safe."

Jonah was used to his aunt's snooty behavior. He responded with a simple "Happy Thanksgiving," kissed her on the cheek, then took her coat into the front room and tossed it on the sofa. Thanksgiving was a revolving holiday in the Bixby family, and this year it was their turn to entertain the troops. Jonah and his mother had been preparing for nearly a week.

Aunt Delia was just making herself at home when the second guest of the day arrived. "Jonah, you're so big. How old are you now, twenty?"

Jonah laughed. Of all his father's sisters, Aunt Gabby was his favorite. She was just as eccentric as Delia, but in a much more down-to-earth way. Her coat looked like it was made from an old rug and her blonde wig could have been on backward, or even inside out. Jonah couldn't tell.

Uncle Franklin and his wife entered a second later and the entry hall was starting to get a little crowded. "Are those Mom's earrings?" Franklin asked. He had just added their coats to the pile on the sofa and was now pointing to two old-fashioned ruby studs on Aunt Gabby's ears.

Aunt Delia seemed to see the earrings for the first time and her face went red. "Those earrings. They were supposed to go to me," she sputtered. "Along with the matching necklace."

"No, your mother promised me the necklace," said Mona, Uncle Franklin's wife. "And then right after the funeral, all the rubies disappeared."

"Well, rubies look better on me," said Gabby with an embarrassed shrug. "Everyone knows that. So…I took them."

"You're a thief," said Mona, which only served to escalate the argument.

Jonah stood in the middle, not knowing what to do. Then his mother finally emerged from the kitchen. "Hello, everyone," she said, kissing cheeks and giving hugs and calming the situation. "Does anyone want to help with the turkey?"

By the time the feast began, over thirty Bixbys had arrived, some from just across town, some from two states away. Nearly every surface in the house was turned into a table. But that's the way the family liked it, a congenial, confusing mass, quite impossible to keep track of.

The party lasted for hours after the afternoon meal, with people watching football and cleaning up or just chatting away in every corner of the rambling three-story house. Before Jonah knew it, the party was winding down and the guests were starting to leave. "The invitation said from two to seven," Aunt Delia commented, as she retrieved her fur from the top of the pile on the sofa. "It's just like the Bixby clan to overstay their welcome."

"I should go, too," Aunt Gabby said and went to find her own coat. "I parked my house in the usual spot. Does my favorite nephew want to walk me home?"

"Sure," said Jonah and quickly bundled up against the frigid evening. As they left, they could see Aunt Delia scurrying up to her black Mercedes. He and Aunt Gabby turned the other direction, toward the mini-mart.

Five years ago, Aunt Gabby sold her house and moved all her possessions into an RV. Now every time she visited, she pulled into the same parking lot a block away and sweet-talked the owner into letting her do an electrical hookup.

It was a beat-up old Airstream, parked in a corner of the lot, directly under a streetlamp. Gabby didn't seem to mind its condition. "I suppose I should get this door fixed," she said. Jonah could see that the lock was broken and the handle almost falling off.

From the second she opened the door, Gabby could tell someone had been inside. Her first reaction was shock. Her second was to check her jewelry box on the bedroom vanity.

"It's gone," Aunt Gabby gasped. "Mother's ruby necklace is gone. If I didn't know better…" She stopped herself and frowned.

"What?" Jonah asked.

"Well, Delia and Franklin and Mona were on my case today about the earrings. If I didn't know better, I'd say someone sneaked over here and took the necklace."

"I think you're right," Jonah agreed.

WHICH RELATIVE TOOK THE NECKLACE?
WHAT DETAIL MADE JONAH SUSPICIOUS?

TURN TO PAGE 82 FOR THE SOLUTION TO "A BIXBY THANKSGIVING."

THE FOURTH OF JULY fireworks lasted until ten o'clock. By the time Jonah got home and into bed, it was well after eleven. He was counting on sleeping in the next morning, but that didn't happen. The phone rang way too early, and a minute later his mom was waking him up.

"It's Mrs. Glower," she shouted through the door. "She says it's an emergency."

Ernestine Glower had been their next-door neighbor for years and had complained every time Jonah cut across her lawn or played his music. Now she lived on the other side of Beaverton and was probably spying on her new neighbors with just as much enthusiasm.

As it turned out, she only had one neighbor, but that didn't stop her. "You have to do something, Detective Bixby," she said as soon as they arrived on her doorstep. "I think Mr. Hemmings killed his wife."

The elderly woman pointed through a side window. "They're always fighting, those two, but yesterday was the worst." She said it almost with glee. "After the fight I didn't see her at all. Then last night he was in the backyard with something wrapped up in a big red tarp. He was burying it. It took him hours."

"You were right to call," Carol said. "Let's go talk to him together."

Fred Hemmings answered his front door and listened as Detective Bixby tried to diplomatically express his neighbor's suspicions. For someone just accused of killing his wife, he took it pretty well. "Mira and I are having problems," he admitted. "The reason you haven't seen her, Mrs. Glower, is that she went to stay at her mother's. I'm sure you saw the taxi pick her up last night."

Mrs. Glower had not seen the taxi. "But I did see you bury her," she said, poking a gnarled finger into his chest.

"Do you mind if we look in your backyard?" Carol Bixby asked with a crooked, apologetic smile.

"Feel free, Detective," he replied and led the way through the house.

The Hemmings' backyard was fenced in, with perfect, long rows of geraniums framing the edge and an expanse of lawn in the middle. The only thing marring this gardener's dream was a rectangle of freshly turned earth, approximately six feet by three, carved into the grass. It looked exactly like a burial site and was easily visible from Mrs. Glower's upstairs windows.

"You must realize how suspicious this looks," Carol said. Her tone was not half as apologetic as it had been. "Why don't we try getting your wife on the phone?"

"Okay, enough of this. Enough." And he marched into the little tool shed pressed up against the house.

He emerged with a shovel and without a word began digging. The earth was loosely packed and it didn't take nearly as long as it must have the night before. When Mrs. Glower saw the bulky red tarp, she let out a little gasp.

Mr. Hemmings took one end while Detective Bixby and her son took the other. The tarp was slippery and heavy. And when the contents fell out onto the lawn, it wasn't what they expected. It was a Labrador retriever, huge and yellow and recently deceased.

"This is Howie, Mira's dog. Two nights ago, he dug his way out under the fence and got into some rat poison. Mira blamed me. That's what we fought about yesterday."

Ernestine Glower blushed and stammered. "I didn't even realize Howie was gone. You usually keep him inside where I can't see . . . I am so sorry."

Mr. Hemmings accepted her apology and even held out a little peace offering. "I have tickets for the garden show tomorrow," he said with a sad smile. "They came in the mail yesterday. But I'm not really in the mood."

"I understand," Mrs. Glower said and graciously accepted the gift. "Thank you. I suppose I should get out of the house more often. Again, Mr. Hemmings, I'm sorry."

On the ride home, Jonah was unusually quiet. "Mom?" he finally said, as she was pulling into the driveway. "Something doesn't add up. I think Mr. Hemmings did kill his wife."

WHAT MADE JONAH SUSPICIOUS?
HOW DID MR. HEMMINGS COVER
HIS MURDEROUS TRACKS?
TURN TO PAGE 82 FOR THE SOLUTION TO "BACKYARD BURIAL."

ARSON 101

"IT'S JUST A ROBBERY," Jonah pleaded with his mother. "Why can't I come along?"

"Because I said so," Carol Bixby replied. She was trying to be more diligent, ever since Jonah had tagged along on another so-called robbery and wound up walking into a grisly murder-suicide. "You're staying with Sergeant Brown," she said, throwing a smile at the paunchy desk sergeant. "I'll be back. Then we'll go home and have dinner."

Jonah watched his mother leave the station, then sighed and settled down on a bench in the lobby. An hour later, he looked up from his geography homework and saw Sergeant Brown pushing himself up from his chair.

"Put that away and come with me," he said with a tilt of his head as he was heading for the door. "Your mom put you in my care, but I guess she forgot I'm the senior arson investigator."

"Arson?" Jonah stuffed the homework in his backpack and ran to catch up.

"Yeah. An abandoned warehouse. I just got a call from the fire department. I suppose I could turn you over to someone else, but . . ." The sergeant was already opening the door to a police cruiser parked at the curb. He grinned in Jonah's direction. "But that wouldn't be fun, would it?"

Jonah hopped into the front passenger seat and asked if he could flip his favorite switch. Five minutes later, they were pulling up to the brick warehouse, their sirens wailing and lights flashing. The firemen were rolling their hoses and reloading their trucks, as the fire chief shouted a hello and waved them through. The fire hadn't been a large one. From the outside, you could barely tell anything had happened at all.

The twelve-year-old didn't have to be told how to behave around a potential crime scene. He entered the warehouse several paces behind Sergeant Brown, keeping his hands in his pockets, his eyes peeled for details, and his mouth shut—for the time being.

"Arson investigation's a special skill," the heavyset officer said, as he slowly surveyed the scene. "According to the chief, the hotspot seemed to be on the second level. The fire could be electrical or accidental, like from a space heater or a homeless person tossing a cigarette. The fire crew already swept for occupants." He chuckled. "If your mom thought I was bringing you to a scene with corpses, my life wouldn't be worth squat."

Jonah followed him through the loading dock and the warehouse space, and then up a set of concrete stairs. The smell grew stronger and the walls on the second level showed more signs of charring.

Silently, they inspected a warren of small offices. There were dozens of them, and Sergeant Brown opened every door, smelling the air for any hint of gasoline, which would have been a sure sign of arson.

"Holy . . ." The sergeant stopped in his tracks. On the floor in front of them was a body, a man in his thirties lying face-up in the middle of the small, empty office.

Jonah peered around the bulky officer and tried to take it all in. The body wasn't burned, and there were no signs of violence—no bullet holes or blood or evidence of a struggle. The corpse was wearing a light jacket and a baseball cap and had an ordinary, blank expression on his face, as if he had just dozed off.

"I guess the firefighters missed this one," Brown said flatly.

"Do you think it was murder?" Jonah asked in a whisper.

"Well . . . he was either unconscious when the fire got to him or already dead. So yeah, it looks like murder."

WHAT CLUE MADE SERGEANT BROWN SUSPECT MURDER?

TURN TO PAGE 83 FOR THE SOLUTION TO "ARSON 101."

THE FROZEN PEA LAWSUIT

"THANKS FOR HELPING," Frankie said as he struggled with an umbrella and two bags of groceries.

It was unusual for Frankie Rooter to say thanks. He was the kind of thirteen-year-old who always told you what to do, who grunted when you did it or else punched you when you didn't. But this time he really sounded grateful.

"No problem," said Jonah, even though it was. Frankie had knocked on his door earlier this afternoon, in the middle of a summer storm, and asked if Jonah would help him shop for his uncle.

Uncle Dexter, it seemed, had injured his lower back two weeks ago and was still in a wheelchair. The Rooter family took turns looking out for him—cleaning his house, doing his laundry—and today was Frankie's turn to pick up groceries at the local market.

"I would have done it on my own," Frankie tried to explain. "But it's been raining all day."

"I know," Jonah moaned. Despite the umbrellas, they were sopping wet, and Jonah nearly slammed into the mailbox as they stumbled their way up Uncle Dexter's muddy front walk.

The house was a shabby one-story bungalow, now outfitted with a wooden wheelchair ramp over the steps. Jonah and

Frankie ran up the ramp and threw aside their umbrellas, only to be pelted by rain dripping through the porch roof.

"*Augh*," Frankie shouted, equally surprised and annoyed by the ambush.

"Frankie, is that you?" a raspy voice called out. "Be sure to wipe your feet."

Jonah and Frankie dove inside the door, stopping to wipe their feet about twenty times each on the inside mat before stepping into the front hallway. Jonah was relieved to see that they hadn't left any prints on the long white rug.

Uncle Dexter was waiting in the kitchen, his wheelchair pulled up to a small metal table. "You feeling any better?" Frankie asked, as he slid his bags onto the counter.

"Not really." Dexter Rooter grimaced, using his arms to push up and adjust himself. He was a young man, thin and fit-looking, with a sharp nose and a few days' growth of beard. "I've been alone here all day, going stir-crazy."

"How did you hurt your back?" Jonah asked.

"In Melman's Grocery Store," Dexter answered. "I was walking down the frozen food aisle. Some idiot must have dropped a bag of frozen peas. Before I know it, I'm slipping on peas and falling. Gross negligence."

"You should sue them," Frankie suggested.

"That's exactly what I'm doing," Dexter said with a crooked grin. "See this?" He reached out to the kitchen table and picked up a freshly opened letter. "In the mailbox today. From my lawyer."

"Maybe it wasn't their fault," Jonah said. He knew the Melmans, a nice family who always kept their store clean and tidy.

"Of course it was their fault. I'm suing for medical bills. Plus a sweet chunk of change for my pain and suffering."

Jonah and Frankie finished putting the groceries away. For all their effort and soaked clothes, they were rewarded with only a mumbled "thanks" as they walked back down the clean white carpet to the door and the porch and the pouring rain.

Later that day, after the storm finally cleared, Jonah sat down to dinner in his own kitchen, waiting patiently as his mother doled out the chicken casserole and brought the plates to the table.

"Mom?" he asked, not sure how to phrase the question. "Can someone fake a lower back injury? I mean, so even a doctor can't tell?"

"Sure," Detective Carol Bixby said, wiping a stray noodle from the edge of her plate. "There's a lot of insurance fraud with back damage. It doesn't always show up in X-rays. Why are you asking?"

Jonah explained about Dexter Rooter and his lawsuit against Melman's Grocery Store. "I think he fell on purpose. I think he's fooling everyone. His family. His doctor."

Carol put down her fork. "Do you have any proof?"

WHAT MAKES JONAH THINK DEXTER IS FAKING HIS INJURY?

TURN TO PAGE 84 FOR THE SOLUTION TO "THE FROZEN PEA LAWSUIT."

DEFYING THE MOB

BRISTOL FOR MAYOR

JONAH WAS NOT involved in every single police case in Beaverton. Being a good mother, Carol Bixby tried her best to keep her son away from crime scenes, especially the homicides. So, on the majority of occasions, when he didn't accidentally wind up at a murder or get dragged along by a babysitting cop or have his mother ask his advice on a particularly puzzling case, Jonah had to make do like every other curious citizen. He watched the TV news and read the papers.

The biggest news right now was the murder of Teddy Bristol, a longtime city councilman. Teddy had been running for mayor on a law-and-order platform, trying to rally the public against the dangers of organized crime. For most people, organized crime seemed totally irrelevant, a big-city problem. And no one took Teddy seriously.

But then came the death threats. Nasty letters demanded that he pull out of the race—or else. Messages were left on his voice mail, promising to break his kneecaps. In the face of this intimidation, Teddy refused to back down. He even refused police protection, which might have been a mistake.

"I'm not scared of some gutless thugs," he told the TV cameras. And his poll numbers shot up overnight. It was starting to look like, with a little luck, he might actually win the election.

That was how things stood on a warm, quiet evening in May when the neighbors on either side of his suburban home suddenly heard Teddy shouting and screaming from inside. The husbands of both families called 911, and then rushed over to the Bristol house. Teddy was a bachelor and lived alone, except for Rascal, his white miniature schnauzer, who proceeded to bark up a storm when he heard the neighbors approach.

Rick Meyers, the neighbor on the left, did his best to calm the dog while John Potter, the neighbor on the right, slipped into the house. He found Teddy Bristol, just inside the door that separated the living room from the kitchen, writhing on the floor, a knife stuck in the middle of his back.

Teddy was still alive and managed to gurgle out a few last words. "Mob . . . killer . . . don't know . . ." And then his eyes rolled back into his head.

The police could determine very little. An intruder had broken a window by the kitchen door and reached in to unlock the latch. There were signs of a struggle throughout the kitchen and into the living room. The single wound was not very deep, only a few inches, but it was fatally accurate, piercing an artery and a section of lung.

These were the facts that the newspapers reported. Jonah read them again and again, but a few things didn't make sense to him. How, for example, did the killer manage to stab Teddy in the back? If the two men had been fighting, then the attack would probably have come from the front. Also, the shallow-ness of the wound. Wouldn't a professional killer use more force? And there was also something strange about Rascal, the dog.

When his mother came home that night, exhausted from a long day of investigating the case, Jonah asked her how things were going. He tried to be subtle and not seem too interested.

"We're checking out all the mob enforcers in the Midwest," she told him. "That takes time."

"Well, maybe it's someone closer to home," Jonah suggested. "Do you have the photos from the crime scene?"

"They're on the department's secure Web site." Carol Bixby frowned. "Do you have some theory?"

"Maybe."

"You know, Jonah, if you concentrated as much on your schoolwork as you do on my police work..."

"Please, Mom. Let me check this out, and I promise to do an extra five math problems from the book."

"All right, young man, have it your way."

Carol went into her home office and switched on her computer. A minute later, she was online, entering her code and pulling up photographs from the murder scene. Jonah quickly found the one he wanted: a shot of the living room door, open to the kitchen, just a few feet from the spot where Teddy collapsed.

Jonah enlarged the photo and thought he could see scratches in the door jam, a foot or so above the middle hinge. It was just what he was looking for.

WHAT DID JONAH THINK HAPPENED?
WHAT TROUBLED HIM ABOUT RASCAL THE DOG?

TURN TO PAGE 84 FOR THE SOLUTION TO "DEFYING THE MOB."

DEAD AS A DUMMY

"YOUR MOM ACTUALLY let you work on a mob case?" Sally's eyes went wide.

"Well, it wasn't really a mob case," Jonah said with a blush.

"But everyone thought it was," Bill Tollbar said. "That's almost the same."

Jonah didn't often brag. Well, not to grown-ups, especially not to the cops that his mom had to work with every day. But here with his friends, in private, it was different. He liked retelling his adventures in crime. And his friends seemed to like hearing them.

The three of them were up in the tree house in Sally Smith's backyard. For the past four years, it had been a sort of informal club, a space that was totally theirs, off-limits to anyone more than a year older or younger.

"I don't get it," Bill said, sounding a little envious. "You're always in the middle of robberies and murders. I've never seen a dead body in my life."

"Well, my mom does it for a living." Jonah stood at the north window of the tree house, looking out over the neatly spaced fences. "So it's not that unusual." His eyes were focusing on a woman lying in the middle of a backyard lawn. A big blotch of red covered her head and chest. He couldn't believe it. "Um, Sally?" he said, trying to remain calm. "Can you hand me the binoculars?"

Looking through the binoculars seemed to confirm Jonah's first instinct. They all took a glance at the bloody figure, then clambered down the ladder and called 911 from the Smiths' kitchen. "Come on," Jonah said as he hung up the phone and headed for the street.

They knew which backyard it was. The Crispens had moved away a month ago, leaving the house empty and unguarded. Jonah led the way past the "For Sale" sign to the side gate and jiggled the latch.

The grass in the Crispens' backyard was high and unmowed, still wet from the morning dew. "Don't touch anything," Jonah said, feeling like the resident expert. "I'm going to check for vital signs."

Jonah was halfway to the body when he realized something was wrong. First off was the hair. It looked like a bad wig. Then the skin: waxy and unnaturally shiny. A second later and he recognized the "deceased." It was Edna, the CPR dummy from the local community center.

Stunned and embarrassed, Jonah knelt beside the dummy. The blood was ketchup, but there was no other damage. Edna's old jogging suit was wet on the top and dry underneath. The dew wouldn't leave a stain, not like the ketchup.

Within two minutes, the police were there, sirens blaring.

Everyone but Jonah got a good laugh at the relatively harmless prank. Beaverton's junior detective, it seemed, had been a little too eager this time, and Jonah was just grateful that his mother hadn't answered the call—although she was sure to hear about it. The officers removed the dummy and ushered everyone out of the Crispens' yard.

"One of you did this," Jonah hissed at his two friends.

"No way," said Sally. "It could have been anyone. They keep Edna in a supply closet. It's never locked."

"No, it had to be someone who knew I'd be in the tree house. This is payback for all the times I told you about my cases."

"You always tell us about your cases," Bill said, still with a chuckle in his voice. "So I can see why Sally would pull a stunt like this."

"Me?" Sally stopped laughing. "I didn't do it. And I have an alibi for last night. I was at a sleepover at Margie's. That's way on the other side of town."

"But you don't have an alibi for this morning," Bill countered. "I do. I was with my family at the fire-department breakfast. Jonah saw them drop me off here just an hour ago."

Bill and Sally continued to argue about their alibis. But Jonah was no longer listening. He was feeling a little better about things now. True, one of his friends did pull a mean, embarrassing prank. But he had just figured out who it was.

WHO PUT THE DUMMY IN THE NEIGHBORS' YARD? WHAT CLUE GAVE THE PRANKSTER AWAY?

TURN TO PAGE 85 FOR THE SOLUTION TO "DEAD AS A DUMMY."

THE LAWNMOWER MAN

IT WAS A SATURDAY morning. Jonah and his mother were just walking into the Cineplex 12 when they heard the explosion. Jonah didn't think much of it. It could have been anything. A cherry bomb left over from the Fourth of July or part of the construction on the Highway 46 tunnel. But two hours later, as they were coming out of the theater, Carol Bixby switched on her cell phone and found two messages waiting for her.

"A bomb in a lawnmower," she told Jonah as she hung up and began rushing toward the parking lot. "It took out a homeowner just as he pulled the cord."

The crime scene was about a mile from the theater. As they pulled up, Jonah could see an EMS van parked in front of a small ranch house with peeling paint. The scraggly, overgrown lawn was made even less attractive by a charred patch at the edge by the garage and the mangled remains of a gas-engine lawnmower.

Carol's partner, Detective Pauling, was already on the scene, and they joined him just as he was interviewing Mrs. Vickerson, the deceased's widow. Her eyes were still focused on the EMS van that was now carting away the remains of her husband.

"I kept yelling at him to mow the lawn," she sniffed into a tissue. "All day yesterday. So this morning, he finally went out to the shed. But our mower wouldn't start." She waved a hand around at the home's general disrepair. Jonah couldn't see a single item that wasn't broken or rusted or covered in dust. "Leon isn't—wasn't—the best when it came to maintenance. So he went over to Andrew Bing's and borrowed his mower."

"What?" Carol Bixby pointed to the blackened, ripped metal. "You mean that's not your lawnmower?"

"He borrowed it from the man next door," the wife admitted. "Without asking, I guess. That was Leon."

The detectives and Jonah all turned toward the neighboring house. It was a mirror image of this one but perfectly maintained, with window boxes and fresh paint and a weed-free lawn. A side door opened directly into the garage, and Carol was surprised to find the catch on the lock broken.

"You think the bomber got the wrong man?" Detective Pauling whispered.

"Looks that way," Carol replied. "We need to get the tech boys in here." She was just flipping open her cell phone when a car pulled up behind them in the driveway.

"What's going on?" A neatly dressed, middle-aged man with thinning blond hair stepped out of the car. In the front passenger seat, Jonah could see a bag of golf clubs. When the man saw the charred circle in his neighbor's lawn, he stopped in his tracks and his mouth fell open.

"Andrew Bing?" Carol asked and waited for the man to nod. "Were you going to mow your lawn today?"

The man nodded again. "Every Saturday afternoon. Right after my golf game."

"Do you know anyone who might want to kill you?"

Andrew Bing turned white as he stared at the exploded

mower. "Um, I am a witness in a big embezzlement case. But the D.A. said my cooperation was secret. No one knew I was set to testify."

"Well, someone knew. And that someone tried to stop you."

The two detectives took the stunned man aside. "Jonah," Carol said, turning back for a second. "Do not go into Mr. Bing's garage."

"Of course not," Jonah said, trying to hide his disappointment. He retreated to the Vickerson property, and after a few minutes of watching Mrs. Vickerson crying on the lawn, wandered into the couple's backyard garden shed.

The interior was as much of a mess as the rest of the property. Old, rusted tools lay all over the shelves and floor. In the middle of the shed was the broken lawnmower, with a small army of black ants gathered on top of the machine. For a moment, he thought he could smell something sweet, like a dessert, and wondered if any of the neighbors might be baking a cake.

Jonah heard his mother calling his name and ducked out of the shed. He walked up to her on the front lawn and said a phrase he'd already said a few dozen times in his life.

"Mom, I think I know what happened."

WHAT DOES JONAH THINK HAPPENED?
WHAT WAS THE CLUE AND WHAT DID IT MEAN?
TURN TO PAGE 85 FOR THE SOLUTION TO "THE LAWNMOWER MAN."

TOO MANY NEPHEWS

DESPITE ALL THE MURDERS he'd investigated in his young life, Jonah got a little queasy when he looked inside the mahogany casket and saw the remains of Kate Olafson. The sight itself wasn't gruesome. In fact, with her mouth closed and her cheeks rouged and her hair actually combed, Crazy Kate looked better in death than she ever did in life.

The elderly woman had lived in a shack across from the park. She was famous for her temper and for the shotgun filled with birdseed aimed at anyone who invaded her yard. Of course, the big drawback of her birdseed ammo was the birds it attracted. It was while chasing a flock of pigeons off her lawn that Kate had her heart attack. She died the next day in the hospital.

"I never even knew her last name," Jonah whispered to his mother. "It was always just Crazy Kate."

"She didn't make a lot of friends," his mother said as she glanced around the nearly empty viewing room at Mason's Funeral Home. "She did mention a nephew. She said he came to see her every Easter. Miss Olafson's lawyer tried to contact him about the will."

"Crazy Kate—I mean, Miss Olafson—had a will?" It was hard to imagine the old woman dealing with anything as normal as a lawyer, much less a will.

"She had a little family money. And she didn't spend much."

"I'll say." Jonah recalled all the Saturdays when his mother would pack up boxes of food for him to take over to her shack.

"Excuse me. Is this the Olafson viewing?"

Jonah turned around to see a young man in a dark suit. "Aunt Katherine," the man said with a catch in his voice as he caught sight of the body in the satin-lined box. "She looks good," he added with a sad smile.

The open-faced young man introduced himself as Kevin Olafson, the dead woman's nephew. Carol and Jonah introduced themselves and offered their condolences.

"We weren't very close," he explained. "But I made sure to visit her every Easter. Her favorite holiday." And then, as if to prove his point, he pulled something from his inside breast pocket. "That's us, two years ago."

It was a photograph of him and Crazy Kate, dressed slightly better than normal and scowling at the camera. They were in a park with spring daffodils at their feet and a hazy crescent moon just visible in the evening sky. "I should have spent more than one day a year with her, but…"

"Excuse me. Is this the Olafson viewing?"

Not only were the words exactly the same, but the man who said them this time…well, he was very similar, a tall, open-faced young man in a dark suit, perhaps a year older than the other. No one said a word as he, too, caught sight of the woman in the casket and spent a few seconds gazing down and paying his respects.

"Hi," he finally said, turning to face them. "I'm Kevin Olafson."

Everyone was taken aback by his claim, especially the first

Kevin Olafson. "This must be a mistake," he stammered. "Or some kind of sick joke."

It didn't seem to be either. Both Kevin Olafsons claimed to be the only nephew of the deceased. Both claimed to have been contacted by Crazy Kate's lawyer. And, most confusing of all, both had driver's licenses that seemed to prove their identity.

"Look," said Kevin Number Two. He opened his wallet and, sure enough, produced a picture of himself and Crazy Kate. "This is last Easter," he said, apparently unaware that the Easter before, his aunt had been photographed with a completely different nephew.

In this shot, Kate and Kevin Number Two were seated at the cluttered table in her cluttered shack. Enough junk had been cleared away to provide a surface for two plates of Chinese food, with food cartons used as serving trays and paper towels as napkins. "I brought the dinner," he said, "same as I do every year."

Carol and Jonah stepped away for a moment, leaving the nephews to bicker on their own. "Maybe she has two nephews." Jonah suggested under his breath.

"No," his mother replied. "One of them's a fake. He forged the photo and the driver's license and didn't expect the real Kevin to show up. This is all about the inheritance."

"Oh," said Jonah, glancing back at the two young men. "Okay. In that case, I know who the imposter is."

WHICH NEPHEW IS A FAKE?
HOW DID JONAH KNOW?

TURN TO PAGE 86 FOR THE SOLUTION TO "TOO MANY NEPHEWS."

GOING FOR THE SILVER

"I'M BORED," said Benjy for the fifth time as he fidgeted and stared out at the rain.

Jonah had been looking forward to today. About twice a summer, he and his three cousins rode their bikes to Grandma Bixby's for a nice lunch and a day in the pool. Like any good grandmother, Pauline Bixby knew how to spoil them, but she also knew how to leave them alone. Right now all four cousins were in the living room, trying to entertain themselves until the summer shower passed.

It was Andrea who came across the silver dollars, stashed in the drawer of a side table. Andrea was older than Jonah, but an inch shorter and rather petite. She let out a high-pitched squeal of delight as she pulled out five shiny Liberty heads and held them up to the light. "Old-timey coins," she said, checking the dates on the front. "1921."

"That's like before Grandma Pauline was born," said Benjy, doing the math in his head. Benjy was the youngest and shortest and heaviest cousin, built like a fleshy fireplug. "They must be worth a lot. I wonder why they are just lying in a drawer where anyone could take them."

"Put them back." It was the eldest cousin, Milo, who had just gone through a growth spurt and was looking forward to trying out for junior varsity basketball at Beaverton High. "We shouldn't be going through her things."

"I was bored," Andrea said, defending herself. "Grandma Pauline always has such cool stuff lying around. I'll bet she forgot these were even here."

"I'll bet they're worth real money," Benjy added. "Like a hundred apiece."

Andrea had just placed the coins back in the drawer when a beam of sunlight fell through the window. "Dibs on the pool float," Benjy shouted as he grabbed his swimsuit and darted off to the bathroom.

For the next few hours, the cousins played in the pool, raced across the lawns, and even found some time to be alone. At around four P.M., Jonah staked out an empty hammock by the front of the house. He was just settling in when he happened to glance at the nearby gazebo and saw something shiny glinting from one of the upper beams.

Ten second later, Jonah was inside the gazebo, trying to see what could be up there.

There was an outdoor chair, positioned right under the beam. Jonah was about to step on the wicker seat but stopped himself in time. The wicker was already torn and would have broken under his weight. Instead, he grabbed a second chair and carefully stood on it.

"What are you doing?" Jonah was so surprised by the voice he almost fell. It was Milo, walking up the gazebo steps.

"I thought I saw something," Jonah said, pointing to a section of rafter. But before he could reach up, Milo was already stretching up to his full height and pulling five shiny objects from the beam. "Grandma's silver dollars. How did they get up here?"

Jonah was stunned. "One of us must have taken them from the living room," he said in a whisper.

"That much I figured." Milo looked very serious. "But what are they doing here?"

"Well…" Jonah was thinking. "The thief must have put them here temporarily, for safe-keeping. We all live just a mile or two away. Anyone of us could sneak back later and pick them up."

Milo shook his head. "That's pretty low, stealing silver dollars from your grandmother."

"Well, she'd probably never miss them."

"Even so. You have any idea who did it?" Milo asked. "Aunt Carol says you're a natural detective."

"Yeah," Jonah said. "I think I know."

WHO STOLE THE SILVER DOLLARS?
HOW DID JONAH FIGURE IT OUT?

TURN TO PAGE 86 FOR THE SOLUTION TO "GOING FOR THE SILVER."

HOLLYWOOD SQUARE HOMICIDE

WHEN JONAH BIXBY heard that his mother was driving out to the Everwood Colony, he begged to come along. It was his latest goal in life to become a writer, and this was a nationally famous retreat. Despite its location in the heart of Indiana, the Everwood was a place where writers from all over went to stay in isolated cabins and work on their next projects—all free of charge.

Detective Pauling was already out front when they pulled up at the colony's main building. "Hey, there." He didn't seem to mind that Jonah was once again tagging along. "That's Clancy Masters," he added, pointing to a lanky man with a scraggly beard who was just now walking toward them. "He's a writer staying here. One of the people who found the body."

"Is he a suspect?" asked Detective Bixby.

"No. He was here at the main building. People saw him picking up his mail."

A few seconds later, Clancy Masters joined them and led the detectives up the long dirt road.

"The area up here is called Hollywood Square," he told them. It was a five-minute walk and ended at a clearing, with four small log cabins centered around a colorful garden. "These cabins are reserved for screenwriters, hence the nickname."

"There are four of us staying here, one per cabin," Clancy continued. "As I came up the road, I saw Harriet Bitterson at her window. I brought in her mail and we chatted for a second."

Clancy's story was interrupted by Harriet herself, emerging from her cabin and munching on a cupcake. The large, middle-aged woman brushed a few crumbs from her blouse as the detectives asked to hear her version of events.

Harriet confirmed Clancy's story. "Yes, I saw Clancy come up the road with my mail. It was time to take a break, so the two of us walked over to Gregor's cabin. Gregor always has chocolate-chip cookies." She flashed a guilty smile. "What can I say? It was a few minutes after noon and I was starving."

Harriet joined them—Clancy and the detectives and the twelve-year-old—as they made their way across the square garden. Gregor answered on their first knock, and Jonah could see the plate of cookies on a table, just inside the door.

Despite this constant temptation, Gregor was small and slim. He continued the story. "As we were chatting, I saw that Darlene's door was open." Gregor motioned toward the fourth cabin. The door was still open, but was now cordoned off with strands of bright yellow tape.

"We walked over to her cabin," said Harriet. "Darlene was on the floor, right by her desk. A knife was sticking out of her back."

The detectives, followed by Jonah, entered Miss Brown's cabin. The body had already been removed. Jonah noticed the empty space on her desk, next to her old-fashioned typewriter. "Wasn't she working on a screenplay?" he asked. "Did somebody maybe steal it?"

Detective Pauling nodded. "Exactly. We think that's the motive. She'd been bragging about her brilliant new idea.

People heard her typing away at all hours. Now . . . she's murdered and her screenplay's missing."

Jonah's mother frowned. "You think one of the other screenwriters . . . ?"

"That's my guess. Both Gregor and Harriet are going through slow patches. That's why writers come here. A million-dollar screenplay sounds like a good motive."

"And there's no trace of Darlene's work? No notes or scraps of paper?"

"Nothing," said Pauling. "The only thing we have is a text message." He held up a plastic evidence bag containing a pink cell phone. "At 11:55 this morning, she texted her agent." He read from a slip of paper. " 'Just finished. Best thing I ever wrote. Talk soon. D.' "

Jonah gazed at the short message and had an idea. "Are there any prints on the cell phone?"

Detective Pauling checked his notes. "No prints. Not even smudges."

"That's odd. How can you use a cell phone without leaving prints?"

Carol Bixby turned to her son. "What are you saying, Jonah? Are you saying the killer sent that message and then wiped off the phone? Why?"

Jonah pulled himself up to his full height. "I know one reason why a killer would text someone from the victim's phone. And . . . I think I know who did it."

WHO KILLED DARLENE BROWN?
WHY DID THE KILLER SEND A TEXT MESSAGE?

TURN TO PAGE 87 FOR THE SOLUTION TO "HOLLYWOOD SQUARE HOMICIDE."

THE CASE OF THE STOLEN NOTHING

"NOTHING WAS TAKEN from the safe?"

"Nothing was taken," the lawyer assured her.

Detective Bixby was confused. This morning a call came in from the mayor's office requesting that she personally respond to a break-in at the Armisted home in the northern suburbs.

As soon as the Bixbys arrived, the family lawyer led them to a wood-paneled study at the rear of the mansion, pointed to an open safe, and informed them that nothing had been stolen.

Jonah could see a red velvet jewelry case just inside the safe's steel door. Behind it was a file folder of stock certificates and behind that were assorted other bags and envelopes and small boxes.

"Why did you call the police if there's nothing missing?" Jonah could tell from his mom's voice that she was irritated.

"Mr. Armisted died two days ago," the lawyer replied. "A heart attack, completely natural causes. I stayed here last night, late, working on the business accounts. When I walked by this room, I saw someone in here. Whoever-it-was ran out the French doors. But the safe was open, just like you see it now. And nothing was missing."

"Maybe you interrupted the thief before anything was stolen," suggested Jonah.

"Maybe." He eyed Jonah curiously. "You know, I asked the mayor's office to send me Beaverton's best. No one mentioned a kid coming along."

"I won't get in the way," Jonah murmured and blushed.

"You must suspect someone," Carol guessed.

"You're right," the lawyer admitted. "There's a stone wall around the property and cameras on the gate. That makes me think it was an inside job. Last night, there were just two other people here. One has a motive but doesn't know the safe's combination. The other one knows the combination but doesn't have a motive."

He went on to explain. "The deceased, James Armisted, had a girlfriend named Tiffany. She was young and pretty and everyone warned him that she was just after his money. But Armisted didn't listen. He even changed his will, cutting out his nephew and leaving everything to her.

"But then, just four days ago, they had a fight. For her upcoming birthday, Tiffany wanted him to give her the family necklace, an heirloom worth over a million dollars. Armisted refused and called her a gold digger. One insult led to another. The millionaire said he would disinherit her completely, and Tiffany drove off that same day.

"James was destroyed when she left," the lawyer continued. "I tried to track down Tiffany, but I guess she didn't want to be found. And then James had his heart attack. Tiffany must have heard about it, because she showed up the very next day. Her first question? Had James Armisted changed his will?"

"And had he?"

"No. The property would have to be appraised and put through probate. But Tiffany still gets it all. So, she had no reason to steal, even though she knew the combination."

"And who was the other person here last night?" Carol asked.

"That would be George, his nephew. George has gambling debts. Over the years, James has given him money and bailed him out. About a year ago, when he discovered that his nephew was borrowing against his inheritance, James exploded and cut him off without a cent."

"And the nephew doesn't know the safe combination."

"He doesn't. I know for a fact that he's desperate for money. But that's the only reason I suspect him."

"When was the last time the safe was opened?"

The lawyer thought. "About a week ago. I had to get serial numbers from some certificates that were way in the back. That's how I remember what was inside. And it's all still there."

Jonah raised his hand, as if asking a question in class. "Did you put all the certificates back in?"

"Yes." The lawyer sounded a little annoyed. "I stuffed them in, closed the door, and turned the dial. Why do you ask?"

"No reason," said Jonah. But there was a reason. And he had just solved the case.

WHO OPENED THE SAFE AND WHY?
WHAT CLUE DID JONAH SPOT?

TURN TO PAGE 87 FOR THE SOLUTION TO
"THE CASE OF THE STOLEN NOTHING."

THE POOLYMPICS PRIZE

JONAH STRAIGHTENED his swim trunks and curled his toes around the lip of the pool. His two opponents did the same, all three of them waiting tensely as Roy Beecher, the park counselor, counted down. "On your mark, get set…"

During the long, hot days of summer, every kid in the area descended on the Long Park Community Center to swim and play and create the same kind of crafts that their parents probably made twenty-five years ago here at the same park.

"Go!"

Jonah dove long and straight, then kicked into the Australian crawl. Once every month, the park sponsored the "Poolympics," a swim meet for each age group. This year Jonah had gone through a growth spurt, and, for the first time, offered some real competition. He barely looked up from the water and made a clean turn at the far end. When he touched the wall, he was surprised to hear his name called out. He had won.

The trophy was small and plastic, but the two other twelve-year-old boys seemed bitterly disappointed at their loss. Brian White even went as far as accusing Jonah of taking a false start.

For the next hour, Jonah and his best friend Sally played foosball. Then they gathered up their things from a row of cubicles just inside the pool fence. That's when Jonah saw that his little trophy was missing from his backpack. In its place was a note. "Cheater!" it said in big, scrawled letters.

"This is so immature," Sally said, shaking her head. "It had to be Brian."

"Or Kyle. He was pretty angry, too," Jonah reminded her.

The trophy was worth next to nothing and certainly not worth making a fuss about. But the single word of the note stung. "Cheater." And this made Jonah totally determined to discover the thief's identity.

Jonah and Sally sat on a stump by the door to the crafts shed and devised a strategy. "We'll talk to Kyle and Brian separately," Jonah suggested, "and find out where they went after the swim meet. If one of them has an ironclad alibi, then we'll know it has to be the other."

They were still discussing how to subtly question the two twelve-year-olds when Roy Beecher, the counselor, stepped out of the crafts shed. "Congratulations again," he said, flashing a bright smile at Jonah. "You won by nearly two seconds."

"Thanks," said Jonah. "Oh, Mr. Beecher, do you happen to know where Kyle and Brian are?"

"Well…" Roy thought for a few seconds. "After the Poolympics, Kyle and Brian both came into the shed and did some crafts. Kyle made a bridge out of Popsicle sticks. I remember he used three packs of sticks and a whole jar of glue. And Brian . . . Brian was working on a lanyard. He wants to make one long enough to be a leash for his dog, although I think a lanyard would make a terrible leash. Both of them stayed about half an hour and then left."

"Thanks," Sally said. "We should be going home, too. See you tomorrow."

Jonah and Sally waved good-bye and started walking the length of the park toward Grove Street. "Who do you think we should question first?" Jonah asked.

Sally didn't answer. Instead, she was staring down into an empty trashcan. Then she furrowed her brow and cocked her head . . . and thrust a hand down into the can. When she pulled her hand up, it was holding a shiny plastic trophy. It was Jonah's trophy. "This is so immature," she said, repeating her earlier observation.

"He tossed my trophy? Now we have to find out who it was."

"Oh, it was Kyle," Sally announced as she wriggled the tiny memento right in his face. "I know that for a fact."

"How do you know?" Jonah was dumbfounded. The trophy looked exactly the way it did when Jonah had won it. Yet somehow Sally knew the thief's identity. "You can't possibly know."

"Oh yes I can," said Sally with a smirk. "I guess I'm smarter than you think."

HOW DID SALLY KNOW IT WAS KYLE?

TURN TO PAGE 88 FOR THE SOLUTION TO "THE POOLYMPICS PRIZE."

WARNING: SMOKING KILLS

CIGARETTES

WARNING SMOKING IS HARMFUL TO YOUR HEALTH

CIGARETTES CAN KILL

JONAH LIKED SERGEANT Brown, the officer who usually manned the precinct's lobby desk. Once in a while, when Detective Bixby was called in on a weekend, she left Jonah with the sergeant for a few hours. The middle-aged cop always had a new riddle and was also pretty decent at math homework. But the main reason Jonah liked him was arson.

"You can't tell your mom I take you to fires," Sarge whispered one Saturday morning as he led Jonah into a burned-out cottage on the north side of town. "But what does she expect me to do?" It was easy to forget that this jovial, heavyset man was the department's senior arson investigator. "Oh, fudge, there's a body here. Your mom's going to kill me."

They had just walked through the home's semi-charred living room and into an extremely charred bedroom. Lying facedown on the rug, approximately halfway between the bed and the door, was an elderly man. And kneeling over him was a crime-scene technician. She had just removed the victim's pajama top and was speaking into a micro-cassette. "Nicotine patch on upper left arm, anchor tattoo on upper right arm, probably from his days in the navy, no signs of blunt-force trauma." She finished her preliminary examination of the torso, then looked up. "Hey, Sarge." She frowned. "What are you doing bringing a kid in here?"

Jonah hated being called a kid. "He's taking a fire-safety class," Sarge answered, with a wink in his direction. "This is extra credit."

"Well, I'm guessing arson on this one." She pointed to the melted plastic of an ashtray and the remains of a cigarette pack on the blackened nightstand. "Someone tried to make it look like an accident, but I think you'll find traces of accelerant. That's something that helps start a fire," she explained for Jonah's benefit. "Like gasoline."

"Jonah, why don't you wait outside?" the sergeant suggested as he opened up his arson kit.

The twelve-year-old did as he was told. He was in the front hall, just about to step outside, when he caught a glimpse of his mother on the porch. She was here on business, he could see, interviewing the victim's nephew. Jonah didn't want to disturb her—and didn't want to get Sarge into trouble—so he hid behind the open door and listened.

The deceased was Alvin Churney, an old bachelor living alone in what his nephew described as a deathtrap, a fire just waiting to happen. "Uncle Alvin had the worst habits," he told Detective Carol Bixby. "There were always old newspapers and magazines piled everywhere. Plus, he was on medication and drank more than he should."

"Did you ever try to help him?" asked the detective. Jonah could tell from his mother's tone that she didn't like the callous young man.

"We tried, but he never listened," the nephew said. "I got back from vacation yesterday. I was planning to come over today and talk to him about a treatment program, but..." His voice trailed off as he gazed into the burned-out shell.

Carol Bixby thanked him, and then turned to the other person on the porch, the victim's niece. She was about the same age as the nephew but seemed much more sympathetic. "Uncle Alvin was a mess, it's true. But he was starting to turn his life around. Just last week I got him to quit smoking, which was a big step. I think I could have talked him into an alcohol treatment program, too."

Carol thanked the two relatives for their time, then watched them return to their cars. "Okay, Jonah. I know you're in there," she said softly and waited for her son to slink out of the house.

"How did you know?" Jonah said, looking embarrassed.

"Because I knew Sarge was here and he was watching you today."

"Sorry," Jonah said meekly.

"It's not your fault. But I am going to give that man a piece of my mind."

"No," Jonah pleaded. "If I tell you who killed Mr. Churney, will you promise not to yell at Sarge?"

Detective Bixby smiled, and then looked puzzled. "So, it's definitely arson?"

"That's what Sarge says." Jonah furrowed his brow. "And I think I know who did it."

WHO SET THE FIRE?
WHAT CLUE POINTS TO THE ARSONIST?
TURN TO PAGE 88 FOR THE SOLUTION TO "CIGARETTES CAN KILL."

ONE MAN'S JUNK

DETECTIVE CAROL BIXBY stood in the middle of Haskell Salvage Center, which was a fancy name for this overcrowded junkyard. She had come here in response to a burglary report, only to find the "victim" not knowing what had been stolen.

"Someone climbed that fence." Pete Haskell pointed to a section of chain link. "I have motion detectors all over. And last night, someone was in here moving around." As if to illustrate his point, Haskell tromped around a patch of yard, nearly tripping over mounds of car bumpers and old tires.

"I live a minute away," he continued. "The alarm company woke me up and I ran right over. But the thief was already gone."

"Maybe the alarm scared him off."

"It's a silent alarm." His voice bristled with impatience. "And no, the alarm isn't broken. And no, it wasn't a stray cat. And no, I don't have a guard dog. Something was definitely tampered with. I could tell. It wasn't the way I left it."

"But you don't know what was stolen."

"No," Haskell admitted. "Look, a lot of this junk is really junk, like I should pay someone to cart it away. But I make a living separating the good from the bad and selling it. Someone cared enough to break in and risk getting caught. I just want to find out who it was, and what he took. And I want it back."

"This isn't your first break-in," she guessed. "You've had the police here before."

Haskell nodded. "My fifth in a month. Always the same. First Sergeant Bingham came, then Officer Miller . . ."

After school that day, when Jonah walked over to the Fifth Precinct, he found his mother waiting in the car. "Honey, I need your help."

As she drove, Carol explained. "Everyone's ignoring this guy. But I checked outside his fence and I found tire marks, like someone backing up a truck. It took me hours to track down the treads. They're the original tires on a 1958 Ford pickup. According to the DMV, we have two suspects in this area."

Their first stop was the upscale home of Kyle Brisbane. Jonah immediately noticed the garage. It was hard to miss. It held eight cars and was bigger than the house.

Mr. Brisbane himself was in the driveway. "Sure, I have a '58 pickup. It's a collector classic," he said with pride, and led them to the far side of the garage.

Jonah was impressed. The truck seemed perfectly restored, every inch gleaming and looking authentic. "Are those original tires?" Jonah asked.

"Absolutely," Brisbane said. "It took years to find all the old parts."

"Did you buy anything from Haskell Salvage?" Jonah's mother asked. "I hear he has a lot of rare parts."

Kyle Brisbane laughed. "You heard wrong. I checked out that place last month. Nothing but junk. He wouldn't know a radiator cap from a baseball cap."

The other pickup owner was not so careful with his cars. He lived two miles farther down the road in an eyesore of a double-wide trailer. Scattered around his property like weeds was a collection of junked cars and old tires and broken chairs. Everything you could imagine including, Jonah saw, a 1958 Ford pickup. This Ford, however, was not in pristine condition. And its tires, scuffed and battered, but with their treads still intact, probably were the originals.

They were halfway across the yard when a thin, grizzled man emerged from the double-wide, holding a shotgun. "Get off my property," he bellowed.

Carol stopped and immediately flashed her shield and announced herself. "Beaverton police, Mr. Klasnow. I just want to talk." She turned to Jonah. "Go back to the car. I'll be all right."

Mr. Klasnow put down his shotgun but not his anger.

From thirty yards away, Jonah heard most of their conversation. His mother was asking about the truck.

"Yes, it works," Klasnow growled. "Three of those cars are in working order, so they're not legally junked. I know the laws and I stay inside them. You can't give me a fine, so get lost."

Detective Bixby tried to explain the real reason for her visit, but the eccentric property owner didn't want to listen. And neither did Jonah.

He already knew the solution to this little puzzle.

WHO SET OFF THE JUNKYARD ALARM? AND WHAT WAS HE AFTER?

TURN TO PAGE 89 FOR THE SOLUTION TO "ONE MAN'S JUNK."

THE UNPROTECTED WITNESS

EVERY NOW AND THEN Detective Bixby's number came up, and she had to help out on a witness-protection case. It was one of her least favorite duties. It meant long hours away from home, protecting someone who was usually scared for his life.

In this instance, the witness was a mob accountant from the big city, Indianapolis. The man had plea-bargained his way into a reduced sentence. In exchange, he agreed to testify against the most powerful crime boss in the Midwest. In the days preceding the trial, Carol Bixby and an assistant D.A. worked the night shift, living in a dingy motel suite, watching their witness and endless hours of bad television.

In addition to protecting Gerald Katzinger from the mob boss, they were also assigned to protect him from himself. Gerald, it seemed, was depressed about his situation and currently under a suicide watch.

Their routine was always the same. They arrived at the motel at seven to replace the day team, bringing with them an order of take-out food from a different restaurant each night, just to be safe. After dinner they played cards with their witness or watched TV. Then Carol made one final sweep.

This night was not different. Carol checked the bedroom and bathroom windows, all of which had been boarded up with plywood. There was nothing harmful under the bed or in the closet or drawers. The razor had been removed from the bathroom and the drinking glass by the sink was plastic, still sealed in its sanitary wrapper, just the way the motel maid had left it.

When she returned to the living room, Gerald was draining the last drops from the last can of soda and making his last complaints of the night to Reggie Harper, the assistant D.A.

"My life is over," he moaned. "The mob has a half-million-dollar bounty on my head. Even if they don't kill me now, I still have to do jail time. I might as well die and get it over with."

"No, you don't," Reggie Harper said with half a grin. "You owe me ten bucks from our little poker game. No one's killing you before I get my money. That's all there is to it."

Gerald let out a weak little laugh, more like a yawn. Then he said good night and disappeared into his bedroom. The rules called for both Harper and Carol to stay awake and for one of them to look in on their witness every hour.

Carol did the first check that night. She eased open the door around 11 P.M. and was a little surprised to see the light still on. "Gerald?" she whispered. "You okay?"

A second later, she saw the mob accountant. He was lying on the bed, fully clothed, his eyes glassy and open, his body contorted in an unnatural pose. "Reggie!" she shouted. "Call 9-1-1." Then she ran to the body and checked for vital signs.

"Look!" Reggie's voice was cold, almost accusing. "How did this get in here?" Carol turned to see a bottle of large white pills on the deceased's nightstand. "I thought you swept the bedroom."

"I did," said Carol. "I swear I did."

The next morning, Detective Bixby was home in her kitchen, fixing her son breakfast and wondering how she could have been so careless. "The pills were a tetrodotoxin," she informed Jonah. "They make you drowsy and then paralyze your breathing. It takes maybe half an hour to kill."

"Are you in trouble?" Jonah asked.

"Big trouble," his mother replied. "Without Gerald, the D.A. has no case. I have no idea how he got the pills or where he could have hidden them. But that was my job, to keep him alive."

The Crime Scene techs had arrived shortly, just before the van from the morgue. They photographed everything, and, right before coming home, Carol persuaded them to give her copies.

Jonah now sat at the kitchen table, examining the photos. "Is this how the room was before his death?" he asked. "When you made your last inspection?"

Carol looked over his shoulder. "Yes, the room and the bathroom are exactly the way I left them, except for the body on the bed and the pill bottle on the nightstand."

Jonah nodded. "Then I think I know what happened."

HOW WAS GERALD KILLED?
WHAT CLUE DID JONAH NOTICE?

TURN TO PAGE 89 FOR THE SOLUTION TO "THE UNPROTECTED WITNESS."

A DOUBLE MUGGING

DESPITE THE FACT that Jonah spent his after-school afternoons in a police station full of cops and crime, this daily hour or so between school and the end of his mother's shift was usually uneventful. He would occupy himself with homework and small talk, or just sit quietly and observe life in the Fifth Precinct.

It was on one such afternoon that Jonah saw a young man, barely out of his teens, stumble in, looking dazed and reporting that he'd just been mugged. Again. This was the second time in less than an hour that he'd stumbled through the precinct house door and reported a mugging.

In the hubbub that followed, Jonah managed to slip with them into the bullpen and take up a position behind a potted plant. From here, he had a good view of the victim giving his second testimony of the day to a roomful of puzzled cops.

His name was Tim Prickle and he assistant-managed a popular local restaurant. During the lull between the lunch rush and dinner, Tim regularly took the cash receipts and made a deposit at the bank. On this particular day, he was sauntering through an alley shortcut, just closing his cell phone, when a masked man stepped out from behind a dumpster with a knife and demanded the deposit bag. Tim said he fought the mugger, tearing his clothes and probably inflicting a few bruises. But at some point, the robber knocked him facedown into a garbage can, gaining just enough time to scoop up the deposit bag and run off.

Tim knew there was a precinct house nearby and ran directly into the station. He filled out a report but didn't have any injuries serious enough to require medical attention. Half an hour later he left, fretting aloud about how the restaurant owner would react to the news of the robbery.

"And the second mugging occurred in the same alley, with the same mugger?" Detective Pauling seemed a little doubtful.

Tim couldn't seem to believe it either. "He had on a blue windbreaker, just like before. It had to be the same guy. This time all he took was my backpack."

"What did you have in there?"

"Nothing much. My cell phone, some cough drops, the deposit slip for the bank, a small umbrella, my gym clothes . . ."

Jonah knew Officer Pauling, and he could see that the detective was having some serious doubts about Tim's story. And then, just as he started to ask more probing questions, in walked a patrol officer with a suspect in tow.

"I saw this guy throwing a backpack into a trash can," the officer said with some satisfaction. "I got the radio call about the second mugging. And then, just a block a way, this guy throws out a backpack and starts skulking away."

"That's him," Tim Prickle said, pointing at the newly arrived suspect. True, the man wasn't currently wearing a mask, but he was wearing a blue windbreaker and his pockets were torn, in keeping with Tim's description of his fight with the mugger. "And that's my backpack."

"I don't know what he's talking about." The suspect was large and stocky and acting rather angry. "As for that backpack, I found it in the alley. The reason I threw it away..." He had to think for a second. "I have a thing against littering."

By this point, Tim had already grabbed the pack and was going through it. Everyone expected that something would be missing. That's the way robbery usually worked, but...

"It's all here," Tim said, sounding disappointed. "Gym clothes, umbrella, papers, even my cell phone." And then, right on cue, the cell phone rang. "It's my boss," Tim said, checking the display. "I gotta take this."

Jonah was as puzzled as everyone else. On the surface, the evidence supported Tim's story. The suspect looked like he'd been in a fight and was caught throwing away Tim's stuff. But why would he mug Tim twice? And why would he steal a backpack just to throw it out a minute later?

Meanwhile, Tim was busy trying to explain things to his boss. "I was going to call you but . . . I was not trying to avoid you—what do you mean? I didn't hang up on you—that must have been the mugger answering my phone. He stole my phone, but he didn't really keep it."

Jonah left the protection of the potted plant and walked straight up to Detective Pauling. "Excuse me. But I think I know what happened."

WHAT HAPPENED?
WHAT SCENARIO COULD EXPLAIN
THIS WEIRD DOUBLE MUGGING?

TURN TO PAGE 90 FOR THE SOLUTION TO "A DOUBLE MUGGING."

SOLUTIONS

SOLUTION TO "JONAH AND THE SICK SWAN"

Officer Oliphant stared, his mouth hanging open. He had heard about Jonah's talent, but he'd always thought people were just being polite about the precocious son of a detective. He never figured a twelve-year-old could out-think a trained graduate of the academy.

"What does it mean?" he asked.

"Well, if you put a period after the word 'can,' then it's pretty obvious."

The patrolman tried it. "I don't know if you want to talk, but I hope you can. 'Force heaven to hate one sick swan.'" He cleared his throat. "This is obvious?"

"Sure. Say it over and over. 'Force heaven to hate one sick swan.' Don't think of the meaning, just the sound."

Oliphant tried it ten times before it came to him. "They're not words, they're numbers: $4 - 7 - 2 - 8 - 1 - 6 - 1$."

"A phone number." Jonah beamed. "He didn't leave an area code, so it's probably a land line in Manhattan, like the postcard shows."

SOLUTION TO "THROWING THE GAME"

It took several seconds for Jonah's words to register. "What do you mean, you know?" Principal Daly wrinkled his face into a frown. "Jonah, you can't just guess."

"I'm not guessing. It wasn't Molly and it wasn't Georgia." This was hard for him to say, harder than he thought. "It was Angie, the center.

She fouled some players, too. And she only made two points all night."

"Angie?"

"Yes. Angie knew ahead of time that the team wouldn't be going to the regionals this weekend in Evansville."

"What do you mean, she knew ahead of time?"

"Monday at six in the morning. Angie was buying tickets to a concert in Indianapolis. For this Saturday. No one would do that—not unless she knew they wouldn't make the regionals. That was her motive, too. She really wants to see that concert."

SOLUTION TO "THE KIDNAPPER'S MISTAKE"

"Who's lying?" Carol asked her son.

"Marvin Granger. I don't think he was kidnapped. He probably just wanted a big payoff from his company because he thinks he's underpaid or something."

"We all think we're underpaid. That doesn't mean we go around faking a kidnapping."

"But his story doesn't make sense." Jonah pulled his mother off the porch and onto the lawn. "Do you think they can see us?" he asked, his voice in a whisper.

Carol looked back at the figures lit up in the picture window. "Don't worry about that. It's light in there and dark out here. The window reflects the light back at them, like a mirror."

"Exactly," said Jonah. "But Mr. Granger says he was reading a book last night. Then he looked out here and saw someone. But that's impossible."

Carol nodded. "You're right. I think we need to have a serious talk with Mr. Granger."

SOLUTION TO "THE TRILBY GHOST"

Ms. Grant was halfway to her car when Jonah caught up with her. "They're lying," he blurted out. "Their so-called ghost must have sneaked up and down the back staircase."

Ms. Grant stopped, her hand on the door handle. "I'd like to believe that, Jonah. But I can't take the chance. Do you have any real proof?"

Jonah thought for a second, then for a second more. "Yes. It was Evan, the son. He couldn't have been watering the garden like he said."

"Why not?"

"Because his father parked right on top of the hose. You saw that, right? So the hose couldn't have been working. His alibi doesn't hold water."

Jonah hadn't meant it as a joke, but everyone laughed.

"A fake ghost exposed by a garden hose," Mr. Smith said. "Good job, Jonah."

"I guess I'll have to buy the house now." Amanda Grant was still chuckling. "This is too good a story to waste."

SOLUTION TO "A BIXBY THANKSGIVING"

"You really think it was a Bixby?" Aunt Gabby clucked her tongue. "Stealing from your own family. Disgraceful."

"Uh-mmm," Jonah hemmed. "Although you could make the argument that you stole the necklace and earrings in the first place."

"I suppose," his aunt allowed. "Anyway, who's the culprit, Sherlock?"

"Well . . . everyone knows your Airstream and where you park it. And everyone knew you had Grandma's necklace."

"But they were at the party. Delia didn't leave until you and I left, just a few minutes ago. Franklin and Mona are still there."

"But anyone could have sneaked out. In fact, I'm pretty sure Aunt Delia did."

"Delia?"

"Yes. She was the first person to arrive at the house, so her fur coat was at the bottom of the coat pile. And yet, just now, her coat was lying on top."

"That is strange," Gabby agreed.

"The most logical explanation is that sometime during the party she slipped on her coat and left for a few minutes. When she came back, she naturally just put her coat on top."

SOLUTION TO "BACKYARD BURIAL"

Carol Bixby put the car into park and turned to her son. "What doesn't add up?"

"First off, his story about Howie digging under the fence. There's no hole anywhere along that fence. Even if Mr. Hemmings fixed it, there would still be dead flowers or some other trace."

"What are you saying? His dog didn't get out and eat rat poison?"

"I think he killed his wife, just like Mrs. Glower said. But then he couldn't get rid of the body, not with that old snoop around."

"Jonah!"

"Anyway, he came up with a plan. He killed the dog, and then made a big show of burying it and looking suspicious. He knew Mrs. Glower would call the police and make him dig up the grave."

"So, what did he do with his wife's body?"

"It's in the house. When Mrs. Glower goes to the garden show tomorrow, that's when he's going to bury his wife. In the same spot. With the dog."

"So, the garden show tickets . . ."

"He needs to get Mrs. Glower out of her house for a few hours. Those tickets couldn't have come in the mail yesterday. Yesterday was the Fourth of July. There was no mail."

SOLUTION TO "ARSON 101"

"How do you know?" Jonah asked.

Sergeant Brown turned to the twelve-year-old and blinked. He actually seemed dumbfounded. "I thought you knew everything."

"No," Jonah protested, a little hurt. "I mean, I know some stuff about police work because my mom's a detective and you guys have been my babysitters."

"Well, now you're learning about fires. It's the first thing they teach you in arson class. Almost all fire victims are killed by smoke. They usually run out of oxygen while they're trying to crawl out of a burning building."

"I get it," Jonah said. It seemed obvious now that he'd been told. "If this guy died naturally, he'd be face-down, not face-up on his back."

"Right. And in return for this lesson, I want you to promise me one thing." Brown's voice echoed through the empty building. *"Please don't tell your mother I brought you here!"*

SOLUTION TO "THE FROZEN PEA LAWSUIT"

"It's not really proof," Jonah said, eyeing the casserole hungrily. He was not allowed to talk with food in his mouth. "Frankie's uncle lied about picking up his mail today."

"You think someone else picked it up?"

"No. He was alone all day. But he went out to his mailbox in the rain to pick up a letter."

"So?" His mother had also postponed eating. "He rolled down his ramp and got his mail. When he came back inside, he dried off."

"But what about his wheelchair?" Jonah asked. "It would have made muddy tracks on his white rug. There's no way he could have prevented that. Unless…"

"Unless he got up from his wheelchair and walked out to the mailbox. Is that what you're saying?"

"Right. When he walked back inside, he wiped his feet on the doormat, just like we did."

SOLUTION TO "DEFYING THE MOB"

"Why didn't Rascal bark?"

"What?" Carol should have been used to her son's questions, but they always took her by surprise. "Rascal did bark, Jonah. When the neighbors came over."

"I mean earlier. When the intruder broke in and attacked his owner, why didn't Rascal bark?"

"I don't know. Are you saying there was no intruder? But Teddy Bristol's last words accused the mob…"

"Maybe Teddy did it himself," Jonah said, almost embarrassed to voice such an outlandish theory. "I don't think the mob ever threatened him. He sent himself the letters and the scary voice mails. And his plan worked. He was getting more and more popular with the voters."

"So, Teddy stabbed himself in the back? How?"

"You can see the scratches in the doorjamb," Jonah said, pointing to the blow-up. "Teddy wedged a knife in there and backed into it. He didn't mean to die, just give himself a wound—something that would be believable and help get him elected."

"And that's why the dog didn't bark. Good job. I'm going to call the M.E.'s office and tell them your theory." She hugged him, then held him out at arm's length. "Now get started on those extra math problems."

SOLUTION TO "DEAD AS A DUMMY"

"I guess it would take a great detective to figure out which of you is lying."

Bill and Sally stopped arguing and turned to face Jonah, like a pair of lawyers waiting to hear the jury's verdict.

Jonah cleared his throat and began. "Bill has a solid alibi for this morning. Meanwhile, Sally has a solid alibi for last night. And we all know that Edna was put in the yard last night. Isn't that right, Bill?"

"Me?" Bill stammered. "You can't know that."

"Yes, I can," said Jonah. "There was dew on the grass this morning. And yet there was no dew under the dummy, just a little on top. That means it was set out last night, before the dew, not this morning."

Bill sighed. "I'm sorry. I thought it would be funny. I should've known better."

SOLUTION TO "THE LAWNMOWER MAN"

Detective Bixby wasn't surprised. "It's obvious what happened. Mr. Vickerson was killed by a bomb meant for Andrew Bing."

"No," Jonah said. "The bomb got the right guy. What would you say if I told you there's sugar in Mr. Vickerson's lawnmower gas tank?"

"Is this true?"

Jonah told her about the ants and the smell of cooked sugar. His mother thought for a second. "Then I'd say someone purposely disabled his lawnmower . . ."

"Knowing that he would go next door and borrow his neighbor's, just like he always did. The killer probably wanted to blame it on the embezzler, the one Mr. Bing was testifying against."

"But no one knew about his upcoming testimony."

"No one except the district attorney," Jonah said. "And Mr. Bing himself."

"So Mr. Bing rigged his own lawnmower?" Carol smiled. "I guess we'd all like to get rid of a terrible neighbor. But this isn't the way to do it."

SOLUTION TO "TOO MANY NEPHEWS"

"How did you know?" she asked her son. "Is it the photos?"

"Uh-huh," Jonah nodded. "One of them wasn't taken on Easter Sunday. So that nephew must be lying."

"Correct," Carol agreed. "But which one?"

"The first nephew. He must have found a picture of Crazy Kate and doctored it with an outdoor background and a shot of himself. I can tell he's lying because of the crescent moon."

"The moon?"

"We learned this in school," Jonah said, sounding like a sixth-grade teacher. "The date for Easter changes every year because it's based on the cycle of the moon. Easter is always the first Sunday after the first full moon in spring."

"Which means . . ."

"At Easter, the moon is always more than half full. It can't be a crescent."

SOLUTION TO "GOING FOR THE SILVER"

"Benjy's the only one who could have put the silver dollars in the gazebo," Jonah told his cousin. "It's a process of elimination."

Milo looked puzzled. "What do you mean?"

"I mean you're tall. You wouldn't need to step on a chair in order to put the coins up there. And Andrea is light, lighter than me. So, she wouldn't have busted a chair if she stood on it. But Benjy . . ." Jonah pointed to the seat of the wicker chair. "He's a combination of short and heavy. He would need a chair, and he would have broken the seat by standing on it. Just like this."

"Makes sense," Milo said, clearly impressed by Jonah's logic. "So what do we do now? Turn him in?"

That was a good question. Jonah and Milo talked it over for about five minutes. Then they took the silver dollars back into the house and slipped them into a drawer in the bedroom, where Grandma Bixby would find them and Benjy never would.

SOLUTION TO "HOLLYWOOD SQUARE HOMICIDE"

Carol Bixby took her son aside. "Jonah, you can't keep coming to murder scenes and solving cases. We're the police . . ." She paused and sighed. "All right, who killed Darlene Brown?"

Jonah giggled, then suddenly got serious. "Okay. Do we think the killer sent the text message to Darlene's agent?"

Carol nodded. "Otherwise the phone wouldn't be wiped clean of prints."

Jonah agreed. "And the only reason to send that message was for the time stamp, 11:55 A.M. I think the killer was trying to give himself an alibi for that time. So, which suspect has an alibi for 11:55?"

"Clancy Masters. He was seen picking up his mail around 11:55."

"Right. I'll bet Mr. Masters killed her earlier—say at 11:45—and took her cell phone with him when he went to pick up the mail. He texted the message at 11:55. Then later, when they all discovered the body, he returned the phone to her cabin."

SOLUTION TO "THE CASE OF THE STOLEN NOTHING"

"Excuse me, sir. Is there a bathroom I can use?"

The lawyer pointed down the hall and watched as Jonah disappeared into a half-bath by the front hall. A few seconds later, Carol Bixby's cell phone rang.

Carol checked her display. "I have to take this," she apologized and stepped a few feet away.

"Mom?" came a whispering voice. "It was Tiffany who opened the safe."

"That's very interesting," Carol said, keeping a wary eye on the lawyer.

Jonah explained from his post in the bathroom. "Before Tiffany ran off, she broke into the safe and stole the necklace, the one they fought over. Her plan was to disappear for good. Then she heard about Mr. Armisted's death. So she came back. She opened the safe not to steal something but to return something. The necklace."

"And how do you know this?"

"Because the necklace case is in front. The lawyer says he stuffed the stock certificates into the safe a week ago, so they should be in front. But they're not. The necklace is in front—right where she returned it."

SOLUTION TO "THE POOLYMPICS PRIZE"

Jonah and Sally had exactly the same information. They had been together from the moment Jonah won the race. And yet Sally knew the answer to this little mystery and he didn't.

"Let me see it," Jonah said and held out his hand.

Sally pulled back the trophy. "You can look but you can't touch."

Jonah thought for a second, then smiled. "I should have known. Touching the trophy is the one thing you did that I didn't. It's got something to do with touch."

"Maybe," Sally said, looking a little less confident than before.

"Glue!" Jonah almost shouted. "Before Kyle took the trophy, he was gluing Popsicle sticks together. Some of the glue must have gotten onto the trophy. That's how you knew it was him."

SOLUTION TO "CIGARETTES CAN KILL"

Before Jonah announced his theory, he had one question. "Are the nephew and the niece the only two relatives? I mean, do they inherit?"

"They do," his mother confirmed. "Mr. Churney had life insurance and this house, which is on a pricey piece of land. Are you thinking about motive?"

Jonah nodded. "If the niece and nephew are the two main suspects, then it has to be the nephew."

"Why? Because he's a jerk?"

"No," Jonah laughed. "Because of the ashtray and the pack of cigarettes by the bed. Mr. Churney had just given up smoking. He was wearing a nicotine patch. But the person who set the fire didn't know this. He tried to make it look like a cigarette started things."

Detective Bixby pursed her lips. "Well, the niece knew he'd given up smoking. She talked him into it. But the nephew . . ."

"The nephew just got back from vacation yesterday," Jonah said with a note of triumph in his voice. "He didn't know."

SOLUTION TO "ONE MAN'S JUNK"

Carol Bixby returned to the car, a little shaken from her confrontation with Mr. Klasnow and his shotgun. "I'm glad that's over."

"Actually, it's not," Jonah told her. "Mr. Klasnow is the trespasser."

"What?" Carol was shocked. "This guy doesn't need any more junk."

"And that's the motive," said Jonah. "He didn't set off the motion detector by climbing the fence. He set it off by throwing his own junk over the fence. He wasn't stealing junk; he was getting rid of it. So he wouldn't get fined by the city."

Jonah's mother thought it over. "How do you know this?"

"Mr. Haskell's house is just a minute away from his junkyard. A thief wouldn't have time to climb the fence, find something, and get it back over the fence before being caught. But he certainly had enough time to throw in some old trash and then drive away."

SOLUTION TO "THE UNPROTECTED WITNESS"

Jonah always liked it when he could help. But this case was even more important. "Mr. Katzinger didn't commit suicide," he said dramatically. "He was murdered."

Carol Bixby looked confused. "Murder? Are you sure?"

"Pretty sure. I mean, if I was going to take a couple of big pills, I would need some water, wouldn't you?"

Carol thought for a second, then grabbed two of the photographs: one showing the pill bottle on the nightstand, the other showing the still-wrapped plastic glass in the bathroom. "You're right. Why isn't the glass unwrapped and on the nightstand?"

"My guess is the poison was slipped into something he ate right before bedtime. You say he had a can of soda?"

"Yes," Carol remembered. "It seemed to make him sleepy."

"The killer must be your partner, the assistant D.A. He poisoned the soda, probably for the mob reward. Then when you tried to revive Mr. Katzinger, he slipped the pill bottle onto the nightstand and made you take the blame."

SOLUTION TO "A DOUBLE MUGGING"

"Mr. Prickle?" Jonah said. "Can you ask your boss when he called you?"

"Go ahead," Detective Pauling said to Tim Prickle. "Ask him."

The restaurant's assistant manager stared at the twelve-year-old, then shrugged and relayed his question over the cell phone.

"He says he called me an hour ago." Tim covered the receiver and whispered to the officers. "That can't be right. An hour ago, I was here, reporting my first mugging. My phone was in my backpack and it didn't ring."

That was all Jonah needed to hear. "I think if you check the suspect's pocket, you'll find he has the exact same cell phone."

"So what?" the stocky suspect said. "A lot of people have the same phones."

Jonah explained the logic, step by step, speaking directly to the suspect. "Mr. Prickle had just hung up his phone when you mugged him the first time. It was still in his hand. The two of you struggled and your pockets got torn. I think your own cell phone fell out. You scooped up the deposit bag and your phone and ran off. But there were two phones on the ground and you picked up the wrong phone. You only realized your mistake when Mr. Prickle's boss called."

Detective Pauling smiled and finished the scenario. "As soon as Prickle noticed the switched phones, it would be over. We could track you down. That's why you waited outside and mugged him again—so you could switch back the phones."